Boris
and the
Missing Monkey

PENGUIN YOUNG READERS LICENSES
An Imprint of Penguin Random House LLC

Published in 2018 by Penguin Young Readers Licenses, an imprint of Penguin Random House LLC,
345 Hudson Street, New York, New York 10014. Manufactured in China.

ISBN 9781524791759

10 9 8 7 6 5 4 3 2

Boris
and the
Missing Monkey

by Brooke Vitale
illustrated by Kellee Riley

Penguin Young Readers Licenses
An Imprint of Penguin Random House

Boris stretched and swung down from his perch. He had a busy day of eating, drumming, and playing planned, and he couldn't wait to get started.

Bang, bang, bang went Boris's drumsticks as he swung over to the kitchen. *Bang, bang, bang* they went as he ate a giant bowl of Sugar-O's. *Bang, bang, bang* they went as he headed for the front door.

"See you later, Major Monkeypants," Boris called to his stuffed monkey. *Bang, bang—*

Boris stopped and looked back at his room. Something was wrong.

Major Monkeypants was missing!

"Major Monkeypants?" Boris called out. "Where are you?"

Boris checked on his dresser. Then he checked behind his drums and in the kitchen and in the bathroom. He *even* checked in the refrigerator, but Major Monkeypants was nowhere to be found.

Boris gulped. Major Monkeypants was his best friend. What if he was gone for good?

"No," Boris said. "I *will* find him. Never fear, Major Monkeypants. Detective Boris won't let you down. I'll solve the case of the missing monkey and bring you home!"

Boris swung down the hall to his sister Bella's room and threw open the door. A stream of bubbles blew into the hallway. When they cleared, Boris saw Bella jumping up and down.

"Laaa-laaaa!" she shouted, greeting Boris. "Want to come jump with me?"

Boris eyed Bella suspiciously. He knew how much she loved to jump, but what if she was just jumping to distract him? He was a detective now. That meant everyone was a potential witness . . . or suspect. Was it possible that Bella had taken Major Monkeypants? Her room *did* connect to his, and she *had* always liked the stuffed monkey.

Boris shook his head. Bella couldn't be the culprit. She would never do that to him. She was his sister . . . his *twin* sister. If he couldn't trust her, who *could* he trust?

"Major Monkeypants is missing," Boris told his sister. "I suspect foul play."

Bella stopped jumping. "Missing? That sounds serious. Don't worry, I'll find him. Let's examine the facts. I'LL MAKE A LIST!"

Bella whipped out her phone. "Okay," she said, starting a checklist. "Where was the last place you saw him? How long has he been missing? Do you have a photo I can show around? I'll—"

"Thanks, Bella," Boris interrupted, "but I just wanted to know if you'd seen him."

"Oh," Bella said. "No, I haven't. But I can find him for you. Really. Let me do it."

Bella liked to do everything herself. Usually Boris was more than happy to let her do the work, but this time it was personal. No one messed with his monkey and got away with it. "I've got this," he said. "Detective Boris is on the case."

Boris thanked Bella and let himself out of her room. Where should he go next? A detective needed clues, but Boris didn't have any.

Boris thought hard. He and Major Monkeypants had spent yesterday with their friend Marge. Maybe she would know where the missing monkey was.

Boris swung down the hall and knocked on Marge's door. "Detective Boris here," he called. "I'd like to ask you a few questions."

He heard a soft *scratch, scratch* as the friendly sloth slowly made her way across the room.

Boris tapped his foot impatiently. He found it difficult enough to wait for Marge on a good day, but now he had no time to waste. Every minute he waited was another minute for the monkey thief to slip through his fingers.

Finally, after what felt like forever, the door creaked open. "La-a-a-a-la-a-a-a," Marge said. "Please . . . won't you . . . come . . . in, Boris," Marge drawled.

Boris stepped inside Marge's home and looked around. The friendly sloth loved to read. In fact, the room was so full of books that Boris could hardly see where he was going.

Boris held up a picture of Major Monkeypants. "This monkey is missing," he said. "Tell me, when and where did you last see him?"

"Major Monkey . . . pants . . . is missing?" Marge asked. "Oh . . . no. That . . . is bad . . . news . . . indeed."

Boris studied Marge closely, his detective radar on high alert. She seemed to be avoiding the question. But why? Could it be that she had something to hide? As he looked around, Boris remembered that Marge's home was full of trap doors and secret rooms . . . rooms where a monkey thief might hide her loot. Was it possible that *she* had taken Major Monkeypants? In his search for a witness, had he accidentally stumbled upon a suspect in the case?

"How . . . can I . . . help?" Marge asked. "Perhaps . . . a book . . . on where monkeys . . . might hide?"

Marge turned and slowly made her way toward a pile of books. "I'm sure . . . there is one . . . over here . . . somewhere."

As Marge ever so slowly turned around, Boris realized that she couldn't possibly be the thief. She moved too slowly to make a quick getaway!

"Actually," Boris said, "I was just wondering if you knew where Major Monkeypants could be. I remember he was out with us yesterday, but I can't remember the last time I saw him. Maybe someone took him when we were out. Did you see anything?"

"I don't . . . recall . . . anyone taking . . . him," Marge said. "But perhaps . . . you left him . . . somewhere. Perhaps the . . . Simi-Plex or . . . the Ferris wheel? Have you . . . tried . . . the beach? I remember . . . we . . . took him . . . surfing."

"Thanks, Marge," Boris said. "I'll go have a look around. If you think of anything else, let me know."

Boris set off to check the Simi-Plex. He found plenty of monkeys swinging from the rafters and even found a drumstick he had lost the week before, but there was no sign of the monkey.

Next, Boris headed to the Daisy-O Ferris Wheel. He searched every car and even took a ride. Maybe the view from the top would help him find Major Monkeypants. But there was still no monkey.

Boris was halfway through checking the beach when he heard a loud sound in the sky above him. It was his friend Tara. "Wahoo!" she shouted, doing a loop-the-loop.

"La-la!" Boris called to his friend.

Tara swooped down, making a graceful landing beside Boris. "La-laaaa," the dragon sang. "What are you doing out here?"

"Major Monkeypants has gone missing," Boris explained.

"What's a Major Monkeypants?"

"Not *a* Major Monkeypants," Boris explained. "*My* Major Monkeypants. He's . . . well . . . He's my stuffed monkey." Boris blushed. He thought Tara was the coolest. He hoped she didn't think it was babyish of him to still have a stuffed friend.

Boris showed Tara the picture of Major Monkeypants. "Have you seen him?"

Tara frowned and studied the picture. Finally, she shook her head. "He doesn't look familiar. Sorry, Boris. But I'll keep an eye out."

Tara flapped her wings and took off from the ground.
"I can see *everything* from up there. We'll find him!"

Boris sat down on a park bench to think. He had ruled out Bella, Marge, and Tara as suspects, but he was no closer to finding Major Monkeypants.

Just then, Boris heard the sound of a camera. He looked up. Gigi was taking pictures. That gave him an idea.

"La-laaaa," he sang, getting Gigi's attention. Boris showed Gigi the picture of Major Monkeypants. "I'm working the case of a missing monkey," he said, "and I think *you* may be able to help me find him."

"Me?" Gigi asked. "How can I help? I don't know anything about a missing monkey."

Boris knew Gigi was telling the truth. After all, she was terrible at keeping secrets. If she had taken Major Monkeypants, she would never be able to keep it to herself. But suddenly, an idea crossed his mind.

"You take pictures of everything," Boris said. "Maybe you accidentally caught the crime in action!"

"Ooh, a crime-scene photo!" Gigi squealed. "That's so exciting! Come on, let's go check out my scrapbook!"

Boris followed Gigi back to her home. Everything in Gigi's house was bright and colorful, and the sun pouring through the windows made the walls sparkle. Boris smiled as he looked at a picture of him and Gigi at the Fireball Games. Now *that* had been a fun day! But her old photos didn't interest him now. What he wanted was her most recent pictures.

"Here we go!" Gigi said, setting down a thick album.

"Thanks, Gigi," Boris said, "but I'm just looking for photos from yesterday."

"These *are* from yesterday!" Gigi said. "I took all of these yesterday afternoon. I can get my morning scrapbook, too, if you think it would help."

Boris gulped as he looked at the size of the album. With any luck, there'd be something in there to crack the case wide open . . . or at least give him a clue about where to look next.

"No thanks, Gigi," he said. "This is great."

Boris pored over the photos one by one. Gigi had taken hundreds of them, but none of the photos shed any light on Major Monkeypants's whereabouts. Boris was about to give up when he saw something in the corner of one photo.

"What's this one?" he asked Gigi.

"Oh, that's me at the museum. I went to an exhibit on the history of cotton candy. Fascinating!"

Boris shook his head and pointed at the corner of the photo. "No, not you. What's *this*, over here?"

Gigi studied the photo carefully. "That looks like Tara. And . . . a stuffed bear? No, a stuffed monkey!" Gigi gasped. "You don't think . . ."

Boris nodded seriously. "It looks like we've found our monkey . . . *and* our thief!"

Boris pointed to the picture. "This photo is evidence. Can I take it?"

"Sure!" Gigi answered. "I print two of everything, anyway. Good luck! Love yaz!"

Boris raced up to Tara's penthouse and banged on the door. "Open up," he shouted.

Tara opened the door. "What's wrong, Boris?"

"You told me you hadn't seen Major Monkeypants," Boris said. "So tell me, how do you explain *this*?"

Boris held up the photo he'd taken from Gigi. "That's you at the museum. And *that*," he said, pointing to the stuffed animal, "is Major Monkeypants."

Tara swung the door open further. "Come on in, Boris."

Boris followed Tara through her house to her bedroom. Sitting on the bed was a stuffed monkey. But it wasn't Major Monkeypants.

"This is Princess Buttercup," Tara said. "I've had him since I was a baby."

Boris's face fell. He'd been so sure he'd cracked the case, and now he was right back where he started . . . with no clues and no witnesses. "Sorry, Tara," he said. "I should have known you wouldn't take Major Monkeypants. I guess I just got excited at finding a clue. It's the only one I've found all day."

Tara put an arm around Boris's shoulder. "Apology accepted. After all, what are friends for?"

Boris swung back to his own home. It was time to face facts. Major Monkeypants was gone. Detective Boris hadn't been able to crack the case.

Boris sadly sank down onto the couch. As he did, he felt something lumpy.

"What?" Boris said. He lifted up the pillow.

"Major Monkeypants!" Boris cried. "Have you been here all along?"

Boris thought back on his morning. In his search, he had forgotten to check the couch! Now he remembered, he and Major Monkeypants had been watching TV on the couch the night before.

"You know, Major Monkeypants," he said, "being a detective today was fun. But I think tomorrow I'll go back to being a drummer. It's way less exhausting." Boris hugged his recently found friend. "Wait . . . have you seen my drumsticks?"